Babe: The Gallant Pig

Harry's Mad

Martin's Mice

Ace: The Very Important Pig

The Toby Man

Paddy's Pot of Gold

Pretty Polly

·DICK KING-SMITH·

The INVISIBLE Dog

ILLUSTRATED BY ROGER ROTH

CROWN PUBLISHERS, INC.
New York

Published by Crown Publishers, Inc., a Random House
company, 225 Park Avenue South, New York, New York 10003

CROWN is a trademark of Crown Publishers, Inc.

Manufactured in the United States of America

Library of Congress Cataloging-in-Publication Data
King-Smith, Dick.
The invisible dog / Dick King-Smith : illustrated by Roger Roth.
p. cm.
Summary: Events conspire to turn Janie's imaginary
harlequin Great Dane into a real dog.
[1. Great Danes—Fiction. 2. Dogs—Fiction.] I. Roth, Roger.
ill. II. Title.
PZ7.K5893In 1993
[Fic]—dc20 92-26978

ISBN 0-517-59424-2 (trade)
0-517-59425-0 (lib. bdg.)

10 9 8 7 6 5 4 3 2 1 First Edition

1

Rupert died when Janie was only two, so she didn't really remember anything about him.

She knew what he looked like, of course. There were lots of photos of him—on his own, or with Mom or Dad, and one she especially liked, of herself as a toddler sitting on the lawn with Rupert standing beside her.

She was just sorry she'd never known him.

1

"Mom," Janie said one day. "How long ago did Rupert die?"

"Oh, let's see," her mother said. "He died when you were two, and now you're seven. So . . . five years ago."

"And how old was he?"

"He was eight."

"That's not very old for a dog, is it?" Janie said.

"Not for most dogs," her mother said, "but Rupert was very big, a giant, really. Great Danes don't usually live as long as smaller dogs."

"What did he die of?"

"Kidney failure."

"Were you and Daddy sad?"

"Terribly."

"Is that why we've never had a dog since?"

2

"I suppose it is, really. We talked about getting a puppy, but somehow it seemed as though no other dog could ever replace Rupert, so we never did."

"What kind of puppy would you have got?" asked Janie.

"Oh, a Great Dane again, I think. We wouldn't want any other sort of dog. But they're awfully expensive to buy and awfully expensive to keep."

"Shall we ever have another one, d'you think?"

"I don't know, darling," Janie's mother said. "We'll see."

"We'll see," Janie knew, always meant "Probably not, and don't go pestering me about it or it'll be certainly not." So she thought she'd better drop the subject.

However, the spirit of the late great

3

Rupert must have decided otherwise, for only a few days later Janie came by chance on something she'd never set eyes on before.

She was hunting about at the back of the garage, where her father had his workbench, looking for an oilcan to oil her bike, when she saw something hanging high on a nail in a dark, dusty corner.

It was a dog collar with a leash attached.

Janie climbed onto the bench and took it down.

The collar was very big, broad, and brass-studded, with a round metal disk attached to the buckle. She rubbed the disk clear of dust, and there, scratched on the face of it, was the name RUPERT and, underneath, their telephone number.

Janie put the collar to her nose. It smelled of leather and dog, and just for a moment it made her feel so sad to think that this faint smell was all that was left of the creature whose great neck the collar had encircled. How many hundreds of times in his eight years of life would he have gone for a walk wearing it, with Mom or Dad holding the end of the thick braided leash?

Janie went out the garden gate and wandered up the lane, the loop of the leash in her left hand, the empty collar dangling. She tried to imagine what it must have been like going for a walk with Rupert.

Lost in a daydream, she almost bumped into Mrs. Garrow, an elderly widow who lived alone in one of the cottages at the end of the village.

"Hello, Janie. Taking the dog for a nice walk, are you?" said the old lady with a loud laugh. Mrs. Garrow's laugh sounded like nothing so much as a duck quacking.

"Oh, hello," Janie said. "I was just—" But before she could say "pretending," Mrs. Garrow put out her hand and patted the air just behind the dangling collar, just where a dog's back would have been.

"Who's a good boy, then?" said Mrs. Garrow. "He's looking very well, Janie. You must be proud of him. Make sure you keep him on the leash, mind. There's a lot of traffic in the lane these days." And she went on her way, quacking loudly.

Some people never grow too old for games of make-believe, thought Janie. That's nice. And two can play at that. . . .

"Heel!" she said, and she walked on, the invisible dog pacing at her side.

After Janie had gone to bed that night, her parents were talking.

"I see Janie's got hold of old Rupert's collar and leash," her father said.

"Yes," her mother said. "She's been carrying it around all day. It's lying beside her bed now."

"When I arrived home from work," her father said, "she was so engrossed with it I don't think she even heard the car. She was walking around the lawn dangling the collar and talking away to an imaginary animal. Every now and then she'd stop and say 'Sit!' and then after a bit she'd say 'Heel!' and walk on again."

"I know. I can only think she must have a very vivid imagination to play a game like that for so long."

"Has she been pestering you to get a puppy?"

"No. It would be nice though, David, wouldn't it? One day."

"Another Great Dane?"

"Of course."

"Oh, come on, Sally!" Janie's father said. "They're awfully expensive to buy and awfully expensive to keep. I mean, these days a decent Dane puppy costs over 300 pounds."

"You know that, do you?"

"Well . . . yes, I just happened to notice an advertisement. And as for feeding a growing pup, well, you can reckon on over 600 pounds a year."

"So we can't afford one?"

"No. You weren't seriously thinking of getting one?"

"No."

"Okay."

At breakfast the next morning Janie's parents noticed that the loop of the leash was around Janie's left wrist as she ate, the collar on the floor beside her.

"Do we have to have that dirty old thing at the table?" her father asked.

"He's not a dirty old thing," Janie said.

"He? I'm talking about the collar and leash."

"Oh, sorry, Dad. I thought you were talking about my dog."

"It's a funny thing," her mother said, "but Daddy and I can't actually *see* a dog."

"You wouldn't," said Janie. "He's invisible."

"I see."

"No, you don't, Mom."

"I mean, I hear what you're saying. By the way, what do you feed him?"

"Invisible food."

"In an invisible dish?"

"Naturally."

"Think of the money you're saving," Janie's father said, "never having to fork out for dog food or biscuits. Can't cost you a penny."

"Of course it does, Daddy. When we go shopping today, you wouldn't believe how much I shall have to spend."

"Invisible money?"

"Of course."

"Has he got a name, this invisible dog?" her mother asked.

"Well, no, not yet," said Janie. "I haven't decided."

"Have you decided what breed he is?" her father said.

"Oh, honestly, Daddy!" said Janie. "I should have thought that you'd have known a Great Dane when you saw one."

"You could call him Rupert," her mother said. "That's what's written on his collar, after all."

"No," said Janie. "I think this dog ought to have a different name, don't you?"

"Oh, yes," her parents said.

"I mean, he's quite a different color, isn't he?"

"Is he?" they said.

"Rupert was a fawn dog with a black mask," Janie's father said.

"Whereas this one," Janie's mother said, "is . . . um . . . well . . . what would you say, Janie?"

"Black with white splodges," said Janie. "Or white with black splodges, whichever you like to say."

"A harlequin Great Dane!" they said. "Of course."

"So he really needs a sort of black-and-white name, doesn't he?"

"Like Magpie, you mean?" said her mother.

"Or Zebra," said her father.

"Or Panda."

"Or Penguin."

"Yes," said Janie, "but I don't like any of those names. I think I'll call him Spotty."

"You can't!" her parents cried with one voice. "You can't call a harlequin Great Dane Spotty. It's not dignified enough."

"He's my dog," said Janie, and she put down her hand and stroked an invisible back, "so I can call you Spotty if I want to, or Tom or Dick or Harry."

"He liked 'Harry,'" said Janie's father, looking down at the collar lying on the floor. "He wagged his tail a bit when you said 'Harry.'"

Janie's mother rolled her eyes.

"Oh, honestly, David!" she said. "You're as bad as she is. No doubting where she gets it from."

17

"Harry," said Janie. "I quite like that."

"Or perhaps Henry," said her father. "That's a bit more dignified."

"Henry?" said Janie. "Henry! Yes, you're right, Daddy. He's wagging his tail like crazy now. Henry it is!"

All this happened toward the end of summer vacation, and as the new term approached, Janie's parents began to wonder if Henry would be taken to school.

They worried at the thought of their child doing lessons or playing games or eating her lunch, always attached to the leash and collar. It was all very well to make believe at home, but whatever would the teachers think?

They waited, a little nervously, for the first day of the new term.

"Got all your school things ready?" Janie's father asked her at breakfast.

"Yes."

Her mother drew a deep breath.

"You're not taking Henry, are you, darling?" she said.

"Oh, honestly, Mommy!" said Janie. "You know we're not allowed pets at school, not even a gerbil, let alone a Great Dane. But he can come in the car with us, can't he?"

"Oh. Yes. Of course!"

"And then he can go back home with you once you've dropped Daddy off at the station."

"All right."

"You'll have to exercise him, Mom."

"Take him for a walk, d'you mean?" her mother asked nervously.

"No, just let him out for a run in the garden. Remember to take his leash off or he'll trip over it. Just let him out at lunchtime—that'll be enough. After all, we don't want Henry making a mess in the house. Especially an invisible mess."

"I wonder what it would be like," said her father thoughtfully, "stepping in an invisible dog mess?"

When, however, Janie's mother drove to fetch her at the end of the school day, she found that she had forgotten something. As they came out of the playground and reached the car parked at the roadside, Janie looked in the backseat and made a little noise of disappointment.

"Oh, Mom," she said, "you left Henry at home."

Janie's mother stopped herself on the verge of saying "No, he's there, all right. It's just that he's invisible." From then on, whenever she collected Janie she was always careful to put the collar on one side of the backseat or the other and to have the leash ready for Janie to clip on when they arrived home.

"Have you told them at school?" her mother asked a few days later.

"Told who?"

"Your friends."

"What about?"

"About Henry."

"No. But I told our teacher," said Janie.

"What! That we'd got a Great Dane?"

"No. Just that we might have one one day. Another one, I mean, as well as Henry."

"What makes you think that?"

"Well, we might, Mom, mightn't we? You never know what's going to happen."

"I do," her mother said, "and we aren't. Your father wouldn't consider it."

"How d'you know?"

"You ask him."

So when her father came home from work that evening, Janie did.

She didn't for one moment think that he'd say yes, though she half hoped for a "We'll see," which would mean there might be a chance, but he simply said "No, of course not, can't afford it."

"How much would a puppy cost?" Janie said. "A Great Dane puppy, I mean. A harlequin Great Dane."

Her father stopped himself from saying "300 pounds." Possibly that's a guess on the low side, he thought, and probably harlequins are more expensive than other colors, and anyway, if I say a really high price she'll forget the whole silly business.

"Five hundred pounds," he said.

Janie looked down at the collar, dangling as usual from its leash, and patted an invisible head.

"D'you hear that, Henry?" she said. "Just think what you must be worth."

"You stick with Henry," her father said.

"I could save up my allowance," Janie said.

"It'd take you about ten years."

"Just think, I'd be seventeen," said Janie, "nearly eighteen, and then I'd be grown up and you wouldn't be able to stop me from buying a Great Dane puppy."

"I'm not stopping you from buying one now," her father said. "Just as long as you've got the money. You come along with 500 pounds and then . . ."

"And then what, Daddy?"

"Then we'll see."

4

Janie's birthday was in the early part of January, and for a treat each year she was always taken to London—to the zoo, or the wax museum, or the Tower of London, or the natural history museum.

"What shall we do for Janie's birthday outing this year?" Janie's mother said to her husband. "Can you think of something a bit out of the ordinary?"

"As a matter of fact, I can," he said.

"What?"

26

"The dog show."

"The dog show?"

"Yes. Might be rather fun, don't you think?"

"Which day? It's a four-day show, I seem to remember."

"Oh, the fourth day, I think."

"Why? No, don't tell me, David, I can read you like a book. Great Danes are judged on the fourth day. That's it, isn't it?"

"Well, yes. I mean, I know they're your favorite breed, Sally."

"Not by any chance yours, too?"

"Well, yes. But I just thought it might be fun for Janie."

"I see. Don't you think it might be a bit hard on the child? She may not be

27

satisfied with an invisible Great Dane. It isn't as if you had any intention of buying a puppy."

"No," said Janie's father. "Though I told Janie *she* could buy one."

"You did *what*?"

"I said that if she came along with 500 pounds clutched in her hot little hand, I wouldn't stop her from buying a Dane puppy."

"You say the stupidest things sometimes. Next thing you know, she'll be robbing a bank."

"Well, shall we go to the dog show or not?"

"Ask Janie."

"A dog show?" Janie said when the idea was put to her.

"Yes. The biggest of them all. Probably there'll be something like twenty thousand dogs there altogether. Of every breed."

"Great Danes?"

"Of course."

"Harlequin Great Danes like Henry?"

"Sure to be some. Though they'll look a bit different from Henry."

"Why?"

"Well, you can't see him too well."

"Can he come to the show?"

"No."

"Poor old boy," said Janie, fondling an invisible ear. "I'll tell you all about it afterward."

Apart from those old snapshots of Rupert, Janie had never in her life set eyes

on a Great Dane until that unforgettable day shortly after her eighth birthday. They had walked into the great hall and made their way past the judging of a whole lot of other breeds—terriers and collies and gun dogs and many more— and suddenly there were the giants, a ring full of them.

Black and blue, fawn and brindle and harlequin, they stood and showed themselves in all their majestic dignity.

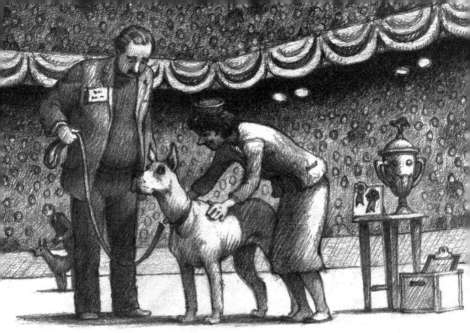

By chance the judge was a little woman, small enough, it seemed to Janie, to have gone for a ride on any one of the great dogs whose points she was so carefully examining.

Janie and her mother and father stayed at the ringside watching as class succeeded class and the handlers stood their charges before the little judge or walked or ran around the ring, the huge dogs striding out beside them. Big or short, thin or fat,

31

old or young, they all had something in common, thought Janie—a great big beautiful Dane.

If only we could have one some day, she said to herself.

A man beside them noticed the rapt expression on Janie's face.

"Bet you wish you had a dog like one of those," he said with a smile.

"Actually," said Janie, "I have. He's called Henry."

"Imagine that!" said the friendly man.

"Henry's rather out of the ordinary," Janie's mother said.

"Out of this world," said her father.

Janie and her parents stayed and watched till the end of the judging, till the little woman had made her choice between Best Dog and Best Bitch. Both appeared equally beautiful to Janie—every one of the Danes there, it seemed to her, were faultless. She couldn't see any difference between them except color. But she desperately wanted the male to win Best of Breed because, just by chance, he was a harlequin. And her wish was granted.

"He's beautiful!" Janie said.

"Isn't he just!"

"They all were."

"Weren't they just!"

Afterward they went around the benches, and there he was with his rosettes and his prize cards and his proud owner.

Janie pushed through a small crowd of admirers to get a closer look. The dog, she could see, knew what a clever fellow he was. He had a kind of smile on his great face and his long tail wagged slowly, majestically.

"He's called Champion Larkmeadow Nobleman of Merlincourt," she told her parents.

"Gosh, what a mouthful."

"But his owner called him Bob—I heard him."

"That's better."

"Funny thing, though," said Janie.

"What?"

"He looked *exactly* like Henry."

5

The mailbox was at the end of the village, not much more than a hundred yards from Janie's front gate. It was built into the garden wall of Mrs Garrow's cottage, and Janie sometimes wondered how the old lady mailed any letters she might write. Did she go out into the lane and mail them from the front like everyone else, or did she stay inside her garden and stretch over the wall and feel for the opening in the box and mail them, so to speak, upside down? No, she wouldn't be tall enough, would she?

One day Janie found the answer.

"Take this letter up to the mailbox for me, Janie, will you please?" her mother had said, so Janie set off, the letter in one hand, the leash in the other, the collar around Henry's invisible neck.

She was approaching the mailbox when she saw Mrs. Garrow come out of her front door, also carrying a letter, and walk across her little bit of lawn to a spot directly behind the bright red box.

She'll never be able to do it. She's too short, Janie thought, but then Mrs. Garrow suddenly seemed to rise higher, and she leaned right over the top of the wall and mailed her letter.

Straightening up, she saw Janie and let out a burst of quacking laughter.

"Bet you thought I wasn't tall enough to do that!" she said. "And nor would I be if it wasn't for these." And Janie could see that the old lady was standing on top of a pair of little wooden steps positioned behind the wall.

"I always enjoy doing that, Janie," Mrs.

Garrow said. "Especially as I always feel somehow that the mailbox is mine, seeing as it's set in my wall."

"Oh," said Janie. "Is it all right if I mail my letter in it?"

"Course it is!" cried Mrs. Garrow with another volley of quacks. "Though I'm surprised to see *you* carrying it."

"What d'you mean?" Janie asked.

"Well, I'd have thought that great ani-

mal of yours would be carrying it for you in his mouth. Some dogs do, you know. My, he's a size, isn't he? What's his name?"

"Henry," said Janie.

"Well, I never!" said Mrs. Garrow. "D'you know what, Janie? That was my late husband's name."

"Oh," said Janie. "I'm sorry," she added.

"No need to be sorry, dear," said Mrs. Garrow. "He's been dead and gone these twenty years, though never a day passes when I don't think of him. And you know what? There's a lot in common between your Henry and mine."

"How d'you mean?" Janie said.

"Well, my Henry was a great big chap, too—he didn't need a stepladder to mail a letter. And another thing, he was quiet, just like your dog. He doesn't bark much, does he?"

"No," Janie said.

"Saw one just like him on the TV, couple of weeks ago," Mrs. Garrow said. "Some big dog show it was."

"I saw it too!" said Janie. "We went there!"

"Did you take Henry?"

"No, but there was a dog there exactly like Henry and he won the prize for Best of Breed. Another harlequin Great Dane."

"A harlequin Great Dane, eh?" said Mrs. Garrow, and she looked down from her perch at the dangling collar and nodded.

"I see," she said.

"And Daddy says I can have a real one,

I mean another one, but only on one condition."

"And what's that?"

"I have to have 500 pounds."

"That's a lot of money."

"It's a fortune!"

Mrs. Garrow looked down at Janie and her invisible dog, and her wrinkled face creased some more, into a smile.

"Talking of fortunes, Janie," she said, "how would you like me to tell yours?"

"Oh, could you? Oh, yes, please," said Janie.

"Come in and have a cup of tea, then."

"Oh, thank you. What about Henry, though?"

"He'd better stay in the garden," Mrs. Garrow said. "My old black cat doesn't like dogs."

"All right," said Janie, and she went through the gate and dropped the collar and leash on the lawn.

"Down, Henry," she said, and "Stay."

"Now," said Mrs. Garrow after they had drunk their tea, "let's have a look in your cup."

For a long moment she studied the tea leaves in the bottom of the cup very carefully.

Then she said, "Janie, I think you're going to be lucky."

"Why? What can you see?" Janie asked.

"Look," said Mrs. Garrow, handing the cup back.

Janie looked in, but all she could see was a scatter of black tea leaves at the bottom of the white cup.

"I can't see anything," she said.

"You've got to know what you're looking for," said Mrs. Garrow. "There's a shape there, all right, a great big shape it is, no doubt about it, and what's more, it's black and white."

"A harlequin Great Dane!" cried Janie. "Is that what it is?"

Mrs. Garrow smiled her crinkly smile.

"I shouldn't be surprised," she said. "And now you'd best get off home or

43

your mother will be wondering where you've got to."

Out on the lawn Janie picked up the end of the leash.

"Heel, Henry," she said. Then she called, "Thank you for the tea, Mrs. Garrow. I hope the tea leaves were right."

"Talking of leaves," said Mrs. Garrow, "this lawn's covered in them. I'd better sweep them up. Bye-bye, Janie dear."

"Good-bye," Janie said.

For a moment she stood in the lane by the mailbox, looking over the wall. On the lawn old Mrs. Garrow was sweeping

away with a long broomstick of birch
twigs, watched by her black cat.

"I'm bankrupt," said Janie's mother.

"And I soon shall be," said her father. "I don't think it's fair. Whoever heard of a dog playing Monopoly?"

"Especially an invisible dog," his wife said.

Janie sat grinning, a great stack of money in front of her. She patted the unseen head at her side.

"You played well," she said.

It had been Janie's idea that Henry should take part in the game. She threw

the dice for him, of course, moved his
playing piece around the board, and collected the rents from all his properties as
well as her own.

She, as always, played with the top hat,
her mother with the flatiron, her father
with the car. Henry's playing piece naturally had to be the dog.

"Okay," said Janie's father as the car
landed on Henry's Park Lane hotel.

"I've had it too. You win, Janie. You and Henry."

"Cheer up, Daddy," Janie said. "I've got a nice surprise for you." And from a wad of money she peeled off a 500-pound note and held it out to him.

"What's this for?" he said.

"For my Great Dane puppy. Remember what you said? 'You come along with 500 pounds,' you said—"

"Oh, no, you don't," her father said. "It's got to be real money if you want a real dog. Five hundred pounds of Monopoly money, indeed—you'll be lucky!"

"I think I will be," Janie said.

Later Janie's mother said, "I wish you hadn't done that silly thing, David."

"What silly thing?"

"Telling Janie she could have a puppy

if she had 500 pounds. You saw the look on her face—she genuinely believes she's going to be lucky. It's not fair to the child—there's no way she could find that amount. Either put up the money yourself or shut up about it."

"I just might," Janie's father said.

"Might what? Shut up?"

"No, put up the money. Ever since Janie brought out that leash and collar, I've found myself thinking of dear old Rupert and what a super dog he was and wondering why we never replaced him. And what with the dog show—well, I must admit I'm getting quite keen on the idea. After all, Sally, we are the right sort of people to have a big dog. We've got a sizable house and garden, we live in the country, and we can afford it."

"You told Janie we couldn't when she first asked you."

"Yes, I know. It's all the fault of that invisible dog of hers. The more she plays that game, the more I find I want to see an actual living, breathing, flesh-and-blood Dane on that leash."

"A harlequin."

"Does that matter? Surely any color would do."

"Not for Janie it wouldn't. And it may not be easy to find exactly what we want."

"We?" said Janie's father. "You go along with the idea, then?"

"We'll see."

"We will," said Janie's father, and he grinned, slyly it seemed to his wife.

"What have you got up your sleeve?" she said.

50

"Not up my sleeve," said Janie's father. "In my pocket." And he took something out of it.

"What's that?"

"An advertisement. I cut it out of the local paper."

"You don't mean . . . ?"

"Yes. Listen. 'Great Dane puppies for sale. Blacks, blues, one harlequin.' "

"Price?"

"Doesn't say."

"Where?"

"Not all that far away. Extraordinary, isn't it? I had no idea there was a Great Dane breeder anywhere near here. And there's a harlequin in the litter. What a bit of luck."

"Janie said she'd be lucky, didn't she?"

"I know. All we need now is for

pounds to drop out of the sky and land in Janie's lap and I shall begin to believe in witchcraft."

At that instant they heard a loud noise outside.

"What on earth was that?" Janie's father said.

Her mother went to look out the window.

"Oh, it's only old Mrs. Garrow going down the lane," she said. "She has the most peculiar laugh."

"I'll say. I thought it was a duck quacking."

"She's chatting with Janie. And she's flapping her hand up and down. Oh, no, I see what she's doing—she's patting Henry."

"That," said Janie's father, "has really

made my mind up. If it's got to the stage where Janie's playing her invisible-dog game with people like Mrs. Garrow, it's high time we got a visible one."

"Will you tell Janie?"

"No, not yet. The harlequin pup may be sold, or it may be a female, or it may be a poor specimen. We must go and see the puppies."

"When?"

"As soon as you've taken Janie to school tomorrow morning."

"But you'll be going to work."

"No. I'm taking the day off. I've fixed it at the office. Urgent business."

"David! You are a slyboots!"

The mailman came just as Janie was leaving for school the next morning. By the time she and her mother reached the end of the village his van was parked outside Mrs. Garrow's cottage while he collected the outgoing mail from the mailbox.

Mrs. Garrow was chatting with him, and she waved at Janie as she went by.

"Funny old lady, that," Janie's mother said.

"She's nice," said Janie.

When Janie's mother got home again, she found her husband still sitting at the breakfast table. He looked rather pale.

"Whatever's the matter?" his wife said. "You look as if you'd seen a ghost. Is it bad news?"

"Well, yes. And good, too," Janie's father said.

He picked up an official-looking document from the table.

"D'you remember my uncle Melville?"
he said. "Well, he was my great-uncle,
really. Nice old chap, never married, came

to stay with us once when Janie was little. Rupert must have still been alive because I remember Uncle Melville made a great fuss over both the baby and the dog."

"Yes, I remember," Janie's mother said. "Didn't he emigrate and go to live in Australia?"

"Yes, and now he's died there."

"Oh, dear."

"Well, he was pretty old."

"Still, I'm sorry. But you said there was good news, too."

"Yes. He's left us a handsome sum of money in his will. This is a copy of it. And he's left Janie some money, too."

"Really? How much?"

Janie's father picked up the airmail envelope that had contained the document.

"Remember what I said to you yesterday? And now here it is, dropping out of the sky to land in Janie's lap," he said.

"You mean . . . ?"

"Exactly. Five hundred pounds."

7

To go to see the litter of Great Dane puppies without Janie, her parents decided,
was now impossible. She must be allowed
to come too. After all, the promise had
been made. If she had the money, she
could have the puppy. And now, by what
they could only think of as the most amaz-
ing coincidence, the money was hers—the
exact money, what's more.

"But we must telephone the kennel,"
Janie's mother said, "and see if they'll keep
the harlequin."

She listened anxiously to her husband's side of the conversation.

"Good morning, I'm inquiring about the pups you advertised. Are they sold? . . . I see. But you still have the harlequin? . . . Dog or bitch? . . . Oh, good. That's the one we're interested in. Can you keep him for us? . . . Yes. I understand. We must take a chance on that. We can't be with you till around four thirty. By the way, how much are you asking for him?"

The answer to this last question seemed to take some time, but at last Janie's father put down the phone.

"The harlequin puppy is a dog," he said, "and he's not sold. The woman said she couldn't guarantee to keep him for us. She's sold a couple of the others but hasn't had anyone after the harlequin yet."

"How much?" Janie's mother asked. "She seemed to take a lot of time answering when you asked her that."

"That's because she was giving me a long spiel about how well bred this litter is, and what the mother had won, and the fact that the father is Champion Thingummy Nobleman of Wotsitsname— you know, the dog that won the dog show."

"So how much?"

"Five hundred pounds."

What amazed them both, looking back on the whole business, was the calm certainty which Janie seemed to have that everything would turn out right.

She was excited, of course, when they

picked her up from school. While they were driving the thirty-odd miles to the kennel, they told her what had happened. She sat in back with Henry lying invisibly beside her and heard about Uncle Melville and the money and the harlequin puppy.

"But he's the only one," her mother said. "He may have been sold by the time we get there."

"Anyway, you might like one of the black or blue puppies," her father said.

"No," said Janie, "it's got to be a harlequin, just like Henry. It'll be all right—you'll see. I know I'm going to be lucky. She said so."

"Who said so?"

"Mrs. Garrow."

"What on earth has Mrs. Garrow got to do with it?"

"She saw it."

"I don't know what you're talking about, Janie," her father said.

"We just don't want you to be disappointed," her mother said.

But when they arrived at the kennel and found that the harlequin puppy had been sold, Janie didn't seem the least bit worried.

"I'm awfully sorry," the breeder said. "Someone turned up a couple of hours after you'd phoned. I did warn you."

She looked at Janie, who stood leash in hand, collar dangling.

"That's a biggish collar," the breeder said. "Have you had a Dane before?"

"We had one called Rupert," Janie said, "when I was very small."

"Well, if it's a dog puppy you want, there are three left, two blacks and a blue."

"No, thank you," Janie said. "We don't want to see them. We have to have a harlequin. Like this one."

"Which one?" said the breeder.

"Janie has an invisible dog," her father said. "He goes everywhere with her. He's never any trouble."

"Sit, Henry," Janie said.

"Did you say Henry?" said the breeder. "Well, I never! How odd." She looked thoughtful.

"I can't say I've ever seen an invisible Great Dane before," she said. She turned to Janie's parents.

"You're set on having a harlequin, then?" she asked.

"That appears to be so," they said.

"Does it have to be a puppy?"

"I don't follow you," Janie's father said.

"Well, I don't know whether you'd be interested, but I do have a nine-month-old harlequin dog that might suit you. He's a good typical specimen, with a lovely nature, but he has a fault that spoils him for the show ring."

"What sort of fault?" Janie's mother asked.

"He's got a kink in his tail—a little sort of twist near the end of it. He was born like that, but I've kept him because he's such a lovable character. Would you like to see him?"

Of course they fell in love with him at first sight.

Already he seemed enormous, with feet like soup plates. He did not squirm or wriggle as a puppy would have done, but stood steady in black-and-white dignity as befitted someone who was almost grown up.

"His nose is part black and part pink!" Janie's father said as the young dog sniffed at them.

"That's all right," the breeder said. "A harlequin's allowed a butterfly nose."

"And he's got one brown eye and one blue!" said Janie's mother as the dog smiled at them.

"That's all right, too. It's just that kink at the end of the tail that's all wrong."

As if he understood, the dog wagged his tail slowly.

"I like that," Janie said. "I want to buy him, please."

"*You* want to?" the breeder said, smiling. "Have you got enough money of your own, do you think?"

"Oh, yes," said Janie. "I've got 500 pounds."

The breeder laughed.

"Well, I'm certainly not going to charge you that much," she said. "Like I said, he's no good for show with that fault. But I don't think I can just give him to you. He's cost me a lot to raise. On the other hand, I feel sure that you'll give him a really good home. So shall we say 100 pounds?"

Janie put out a hand.

"It's a deal," she said. "What's he called?"

"You aren't going to believe it," the breeder said. "In fact, I must confess that

there's something very strange about all this. But he's called Henry."

Janie nodded. It was as though she had expected this news.

Carefully she unbuckled the collar from the invisible dog and fastened it around the neck of his successor.

"Good boy, Henry," she said.

About a week later Janie came out of the front gate and turned up the lane, the leash in her left hand, her dog walking steadily at heel with his long strides, his great head not far below her shoulder. From the buckle of his collar hung a new round metal disk that said, above the telephone number, HENRY.

They walked through the village until they came to Mrs. Garrow's wall with the red mailbox built into it. Janie opened the garden gate and went in.

Inside the porch of the cottage were Mrs. Garrow's galoshes and, leaning in the corner, the long broomstick that she used for sweeping up leaves.

Her cat sat on the mat.

"My old black cat doesn't like dogs," Mrs. Garrow had said, but to Janie's surprise the cat stood up and began to rub itself against one of Henry's long legs, purring loudly. Henry looked embarrassed.

Janie knocked on the front door, and after a moment old Mrs. Garrow opened it, smiling her crinkly smile.

"Hello," Janie said. "This is Henry."

"I know that, dear," said Mrs. Garrow. "You showed him to me before, lots of times. Don't you remember?"

She patted the dog.

"Who's a good boy, then?" she said. "He's looking very well, Janie. You must be proud of him."

"I am," Janie said. "D'you know, he's got a butterfly nose—"

"And different-colored eyes and a twist in the tail," said Mrs. Garrow. "It was all in the tea leaves."

"How could you know all that?" said Janie.

Mrs. Garrow let out her usual volley of quacks.

"Aha, Janie my dear," she said. "That's the twist in the tale."

DICK KING-SMITH was born and raised in Gloucestershire, England. He served in the Grenadier Guards during World War II, then returned home to Gloucestershire, to realize his lifelong ambition of farming. After twenty years as a farmer, he turned to teaching and then to writing the children's books that have earned him many fans on both sides of the Atlantic. Inspiration for his writing comes from his farm and his animals.

Among his well-loved novels are *Babe: The Gallant Pig, Harry's Mad, Martin's Mice* (each an American Library Association Notable Book); *Ace: The Very Important Pig* (a *School Library Journal* Best Book of the Year); *The Toby Man, Paddy's Pot of Gold,* and *Pretty Polly*. Additional honors and awards he has received are a *Boston Globe–Horn Book* Award (for *Babe: The Gallant Pig*) and the California Young Reader Medal (for *Harry's Mad*). In 1992, he was named Children's Author of the Year at the British Book Awards.